Spillthrou

Daniel F. Galouye

Alpha Editions

This edition published in 2024

ISBN : 9789361470394

Design and Setting By
Alpha Editions
www.alphaedis.com
Email - info@alphaedis.com

As per information held with us this book is in Public Domain.
This book is a reproduction of an important historical work. Alpha Editions uses the best technology to reproduce historical work in the same manner it was first published to preserve its original nature. Any marks or number seen are left intentionally to preserve its true form.

SPILLTHROUGH

By Daniel F. Galouye

> Ships switching from hyper to normal space had to do it in a microsecond—if the crews were to live. But it would take Brad suicidal minutes!

Like the sibilant, labored breathing of a dying monster, the tortured ship wailed its death sobs as it floundered in deep hyperstellar space.

Clank-sss, clank-sss, went the battered safety valve of the pile cooling system.

BOOM ... *boom* ... BOOM ... *boom*. A severed and dangling piston rod crashed in monotonous rhythm against a deck beam as the rest of the auxiliary compression unit strained to satisfy its function.

An off-beat bass viol strum added its depressive note to the symphony of destruction's aftermath—*throom-throom* ... *throom-throom*. It was the persistent expansion of plate metal reacting to heat from a ruptured tube jacket.

Forward, in the control compartment of the cargo craft, the sounds were muted. But the intervening bulkheads did not lessen their portent.

Brad Conally ran a hand over the stubbles on his cheek and swayed forward in the bucket-type seat, his head falling to rest against the control column.

Somewhere aft the ship groaned and metal scraped against metal with a sickening rending sound.

There was a lurch and Brad was jerked to one side, his head ramming against the inclination control. The ventral jet came to life in unexpected protest and fired once.

His hand shot out instinctively to return the loose, displaced lever to neutral. But the force of the single burst had already taken effect and the lower part of his stomach tied itself in a knot.

Centrifugal force reeled him to the fringe of consciousness. He struggled to reach the dorsal-ventral firing lever, praying that the linkage was not severed and the mechanism was still operative. His hand found the lever and jerked. The dorsal jet came to life with a roar. He jockeyed the control back and forth across neutral position. The two jets fired alternately. The sickening, end-over-end gyration became gentler.

The ship steadied itself again into immobility. But a snap sounded from back aft. It was followed by a grating noise that crescendoed and culminated in a terrific crash. His ears popped. A *clang* reverberated, evidence of an automatic airlock sealing off another punctured section of the vessel.

Shrugging fatigue from his body, he looked up at the panel. The massometer showed a decrease of six tons. The explanation was simple, Brad laughed dryly: A good one-quarter of his load of crated inter-calc audio retention banks had rammed through the hull and floated into space.

He glanced at the scope. The twenty odd crates, some of them taking up an orbital relationship with the vessel, were blips on the screen.

Twisting the massometer section selector, he read off the figures. Hold One showed full cargo of inter-calc equipment. Hold Two, with its thirty bins of hematite, was intact. The third cargo compartment, containing more crated inter-calc units, was the damaged one. The massometer reading for that hold accounted for the missing weight.

"How're you doing, Brad?" the receiver rasped feebly. He recoiled at the unexpected sound.

"She's still in one piece, Jim," he shouted to compensate for the strength the signal would lose in traveling the distance to the fleeing lifecraft. "Have you cleared through your second hyperjump yet?"

"Getting ready to go into the third. There won't be any more communicating after that ... not with this short-range gear and your faulty transmitter. Find out the trouble yet?"

Brad ignored the question. "How long, Jim?" His voice was eager. "How long before you get to port?"

"Three jumps in one day. Seven more to go. That figures out to a little over two more days. I'm making better time than we expected with this peanut. Allow two more days for the slow tows to return.... Still think it'll hold together?"

Brad was silent.

"Brad," Jim's voice went into low gear. "I've still got enough juice to come back and pick you up. After all, one ship and one load of cargo ... it's just not worth it."

Brad listened to the ominous convulsions of the ship for a moment. "Your orders are to continue to Vega IV. I'm sticking."

"But, skipper! Dammit! There's always the chance of spilling through into normal! That's a torturous way to go!"

Brad's lips brushed roughly against the bulkhead mike. "If I fall through it's just me, isn't it?"

Although the sound level was too low, he knew there was a sigh on the other end. "Okay," the speaker whispered. "If I can't convince you...."

Brad leaned against the bulkhead and shivered. He'd have to see whether he couldn't get more output from the heat converter—if he could chance going past the leaking pile again. Or *was* it the cold that was causing him to tremble?—If he entered normal space at less than minimum breakthrough speed.... He didn't complete the distasteful mental picture.

He thought of his only functioning hyperdrive tube. Its gauge showed a power level that was only high enough to boost the craft back onto the hyperspace level when it started to conform with the normal tendency to fall through. How many times the tube could be counted on to repeat the performance he couldn't guess. It might be painful if he should let the drop gain too much momentum before correcting—human beings were built to cross the barrier in nothing longer than a micro-second. But, he resolved, he would worry about that when the time came.

"Why don't you let it go, Brad?" the voice leaped through the grating again.

Brad started. He thought Jim had cut the communication.

"You know the score. If we swing this we can get all of West Cluster Supplies' work. We'll need an extra ship—several of them. But with the contract we'll be able to borrow as much as we want."

Jim laughed. "At least I'm glad there's a rational, mercenary motive. For a while I thought you were going through with that go-down-with-the-ship routine."

Boom ... *Boom* ... BOOM. The loose rod pounded with suddenly increasing fury.

He lunged through the hatch. At least the compression unit was forward of the faulty pile. And, while he did the job which automatic regulators had abandoned, he would not have to keep track of his time of exposure to hard radiation.

"Calling Space Ship Fleury. Repeat: Calling Space Ship Fleury.... Answer please."

Brad jerked his head off the panel ledge. Hot coffee from a container that his limp hand half-gripped sloshed over the brim and spilled on the deck. He turned a haggard, puzzled face to the bulkhead speaker.

It had flooded the compartment with sound—live, vibrant sound. The signal had been loud and clear. Not weak. Not like the one from Jim's lifecraft two jumps away.

"This is the SS Fleury!" he shouted, stumbling forward eagerly and gripping the gooseneck of the mike. "Come in!"

"Fleury from SS Cluster Queen.... Answering your SOS."

His hopes suddenly vanished. "Is that Altman? What are you doing on this run?"

"Yeah, Conally. This is Altman. Freeholding to Vega.... What's your trouble? Anything serious?"

Altman had come in to unload at Arcturus II Spaceport while the Fleury was still docked, Brad recalled. The huge ship had been berthed next to his.

"Main drive jacket blown out in the engine compartment," Brad said hoarsely. "It happened at the end of the eighth jump. We're about a half-notch into hyper—just barely off the border."

"That's tough." There was little consolation in the tone. "Got any passengers?"

"No. None this trip. I'm solo now. My engineer's gone off in the craft."

"Can't you replace that jacket and limp through?"

"Got a faulty gasket on the replacement. Can't be patched up."

"You're in a helluva fix, Conally. Even a Lunar ferry pilot's got enough sense to check his spare parts before blastoff."

"I check mine after each landing. There isn't much that can happen to it when the pile's cold.... Can you give me a tow, Altman?"

"Can't do that, Conally. I'm not...."

"If you'll just give me a boost then. To the crest of this hyperjump. Then I won't have to worry about slipping through."

"Like I started to tell you," Altman intoned insistently, "one of my grapples is sheared."

"You still have two more."

"Uh-uh. This wise boy ain't gonna take a chance of a line snapping and knocking a hunk outta my hull. Especially when you got cargo spilling all over space."

Brad clenched his fists. He spoke through his teeth. "Look, Altman. Regulations say...."

"... I gotta help you," the other cut him short. "I know that, pal. That's why I happen to be stopping off at this not too enticing spot. And I'm offering help.... Come aboard any time you want."

"And hang up a free salvage sign on the Fleury?"

Altman didn't answer.

Twisting the gooseneck in his hand, Brad sucked in a deep breath and blew it out in a rush. But he didn't say what had leaped into his mind. Instead he glanced over at the panel's screen.

Altman's ship showed up there—a large, greenish-yellow blip. There were other small dots on the scope too. As he looked, the large blip coasted over to one of the dots. The two became one mark on the screen.

"You're picking up my cargo!" Brad shouted.

"The stuff not in orbit around the Fleury ain't yours any longer, Conally," Altman laughed. "You oughta bone up on your salvage laws."

"You damned scavenger!"

"Now, now, Brad," the other said smoothly. "What would you do if you were in my position? Would you let top priority cargo slip through to normal and get lost off the hyperlane? Or would you scoop it up and bring it in for bonus price?"

"You're not after a bonus," Brad roared into the mike. "You're after a contract.... Altman, I'll pay two thousand for a ten-minute tow up-arc. That'll almost wipe out my profit on this haul."

"No sale."

Brad gripped the mike with both hands. "So you're just going to sit around and pick up cargo droppings!"

"The book says I gotta stick around until you come aboard, until you get underway on hyperpower, or until there just ain't any more ship or crew.... Might as well pick up cargo; there's nothing else to do."

"And when I come aboard you'll want to unload the Fleury too, I take it."

"Wouldn't you?"

Half the spilled crates were in close orbit around the SS Fleury. The tri-D scope showed that. Brad estimated distances of several of the objects as he clamped the helmet to the neckring of his suit and clattered to the pilot compartment airlock.

In the lock he unsnapped the hand propulsor from its bulkhead niche and clamped it to his wrist plate while the outer hatch swung open and the lock's air exploded into a void encrusted with a crisscross of vivid, vari-colored lines. The individual streaks, he estimated, averaged at least ten degrees in length. That indicated he was a reasonable period of time away from spillthrough into normal space where the lines would compress into the myriad normal pinpoints that were stars, undistorted by hyperspace perspective. When the streaks decreased to four or five degrees, he reminded himself, that was the time to start worrying about dropping out the bottom of the trough.

He waited until one of the square, tumbling objects rolled by, obscuring sections of the out-of-focus celestial sphere as it whirled in its orbit. Timing it, he waited for the box to complete another revolution. Just before it arrived the third time, he pushed off.

As he closed in on the crate, he knew his timing had been correct. He intercepted it directly above the hatch and clung clumsily to a hand ring as its greater mass swept him along in an altered orbit. A quick blast from his propulsor eliminated the rotation he had imparted to the object and he reoriented himself with respect to the ship. Spotting the ruptured sideplate where the cargo had burst through the hull, he steered his catch toward the hole with short bursts of power.

The bent plate made a natural ramp down which he slid the crate onto the gravity-fluxed deck. Inside, he degravitated the chamber, floated the box into position and double-lashed it to the deck.

Pushing away from the ship again, he checked the length of the stellar grid streaks. They were still approximately ten degrees long. It looked hopeful. He might have time to collect all the orbiting cargo before he got dangerously close to spillthrough. Then he'd see about pushing on up-arc until the fuzzy streaks stretched to forty or fifty degrees—perhaps even ninety, if he could allow himself the luxury of wishful thinking. There he'd be at quartercrest and would have time to rest before worrying about being drawn down the arc again toward normal space.

While he jockeyed the fourth crate into the hold, a huge shadow suddenly blotched out part of the star lines off to the port side. It was the Cluster Queen pursuing a crate not in orbit around the Fleury. Brad shrugged; he'd be unable to pick up the ones that far out anyway.

But his head jerked upright in the helmet suddenly. If Altman was after a free box, he realized, the Cluster Queen *could not* appear in sharp outline to an observer in the Fleury system! The Fleury, sliding down the hyperspatial arc with its orbiting crates, would be moving slowly toward normal space in response to the interdimensional pull exerted by its warp flux rectifier, hidden inaccessibly in the bowels of the pile, as it was on most outdated ships. But the free boxes, in another time-space system with the Cluster Queen, would be stationary on the arc and would appear increasingly fuzzy as the planal displacement between the two systems became greater.

The truth, Brad realized, was that the Cluster Queen was drawing closer both spatially and on the descending node of the hyperspatial arc! Altman was violating the law; he was going to take the cargo in orbit. And he could well get away with it too, since it would be the word of only one man aboard the Fleury against the word of the entire crew of the Queen.

There were still six boxes in orbit. He pushed out again toward the closest and saw he had not been wrong in his reasoning. The Queen's outline was razor-edge sharp; it was close enough to stretch across fifty-five degrees of the celestial sphere.

He kept it in the corner of his vision as he hooked on to the crate and started back to the ship. The Queen was reversing attitude slowly. When he had first spotted it, it was approaching at an angle, nose forward. But now it had gyroed broadside and was continuing to turn as it drifted slowly toward Brad and the box.

"Altman!" he cried into his all-wave helmet mike. "You're on collision course!"

Brad kicked away from the crate and streaked back toward the Fleury.

There was a laugh in the receiver. "Did you hear something, Bronson?"

"No, captain," another voice laughed. "For a moment I thought maybe I picked up a small blip near that crate. But I don't guess Conally would be stupid enough to suit up and try to hustle his own cargo."

Brad activated his propulsor again and gained impetus in his dash for the Fleury's hatch.

"Still," Altman muttered, "it seems like I heard somebody say something about a collision course."

The Cluster Queen was no longer turning. It had stabilized, with its tubes pointed in the general direction of the Fleury and her floating crates.

Perspiration formed on Brad's forehead as he glanced up and saw the other ship steady itself, settling on a predetermined, split-hair heading. Somebody, he realized grimly, was doing a good job of aiming the vessel's stern.

He got additional speed out of his propulsor, but the tubes swung slowly as he covered more of the distance to his hatch. It seemed he couldn't escape his position of looking up into the mouths of the jets.

"I don't know, boss," the speaker near his ear sounded again. "Maybe he *is* out there."

"We better not take chances, then," Altman was not hiding the heavy sarcasm in his words. "Blast away!"

Brad kicked sideways, stiffened his arm and hit the wrist jet full force. He shot to one side on a course parallel with the Fleury.

A blinding gusher of raw energy exploded—a cone of blistering, scintillating force that streaked through space between himself and the disabled ship. The aiming was perfect. Had he not swerved off when he did, had he stayed on his original course, he would have been in the center of the lance of hell-power.

As he drifted shakily into the hatch, the Queen wasn't even a dot against the trellis of star traces. But, while he looked, a miniature lance of flame burst in the general direction in which Altman's vessel had gone—scores of miles away. He was maneuvering a standard turn to approach again, Brad realized.

If he repeated the performance against the hull of the Fleury, he would shake things up considerably, but at least the alloys of the plates could stand the heat—possibly the thrust too ... but not for long.

Invigorating effects of hot coffee flowed through Brad as he sat strapped in the pilot's seat and allowed himself the luxury of a cigarette.

But his eyes were fastened on the screen. The Cluster Queen was drawing up to the last orbiting crate. He watched the large blip and the dot become one.

Abruptly, there was motion in the direct-view port overhead. The Queen and the crate drifted into view. He switched his gaze from the screen and watched grapples clamp the crate like giant mandibles, drawing it into the Queen.

His chest and abdomen hurt and he wanted to get out of the seat and stretch, move around, do something. But that might be disastrous. If Altman was going to play any more tricks with his tubes, he would be ready to do it now, after the last box had been retrieved. And Brad realized it wouldn't be healthy being shaken around inside an erratically spinning compartment.

"That's the last one, Altman," he spoke dully into the mike.

"Say!" The irony was still in the other's voice. "Were you out there when we blasted to avoid collision?"

Brad said nothing.

"Sorry if we warmed your tail," Altman continued. "But you should'a stayed inside. Our instruments show you're getting close to spillthrough. Ain't you gonna do anything about it?"

Brad snapped to alertness. Now he realized the origin of the pains in his stomach and chest—the pin-prick sensations that seemed to be spreading throughout his flesh. He glanced out the direct-view port. Altman was right. The sky was no longer a grid of star streaks. The lines had shrunken; their lengths now stretched scarcely over three or four degrees. The scope showed the Queen was still there spatially, but the fuzziness of her outline indicated she was well out of danger—high up on the ascending node of the arc.

"What's on the program, Altman?" Brad asked bitterly. "Let me guess.... I slip through the barrier. Passage at slow speed makes pretty much of a pulpy mess out of my body. You pop the Queen through in a millisecond.... You got a nice story to tell: You arrived as I was slipping through. You couldn't do anything to stop me. You plunged through after me. With a dead skipper aboard, the ship and cargo were free to the first one who came along. You took the cargo, it being high priority stuff. You left the ship, it being outdated, battered, useless and drifting in normal interstellar where it would never be found. You took what was left of the skipper, it being good evidence to substantiate your tale."

"Now Brad, boy!" Altman stretched the words out in mock reprimand. "You know *I* wouldn't do a thing like *that*. You know the West Cluster contract doesn't mean *that* much to *me*!"

There was a long silence. Apparently Altman wasn't going to interrupt it. Brad looked back at the scope. The Queen had withdrawn spatially and hyperspatially.

The pains in his body rose sharply and he grimaced, biting down on his lips. A knife slipped into his abdomen, twisted and shot up through his chest and into his head. Then an incendiary bomb went off somewhere in his stomach.

He reached for the control of the good main hyperjet. Then, as his face contorted with near agony, he punched down on it.

The pain left swiftly. The ship rattled and clanked and ground hatefully, its new cacophony of protest drowning out the old *clank-sss*, *boom* and *throom-throom*. The small blurs in the sky elongated—five degrees, ten, twelve, twenty, twenty-five, forty.... The Cluster Queen's outline on the scope became sharp and then faded into fuzziness once more as the Fleury passed it hyperspatially along the ascending node of the arc.

He pressed the normal drive jet lever and it spluttered weakly, creating not even enough discordant sounds in the wracked ship to drown out the *boom*, *throom*, *clank-sss* symphony. The dot on the scope representing the Queen faded into insignificance. With a sweep of his hand, he killed power in the automatic distress transmitter.

Now it would take the Queen a little while to get a bearing on him along four co-ordinates. It would be a reprieve of several' hours—even the Fleet ships couldn't do it in less time than that without a signal to home in on.

He had no idea what the skipper of the Queen would do next. But at the moment he wasn't interested. The sharp pains were gone. But they had been replaced by an uncontrollable, reactive nausea. He unclamped his safety harness and stumbled to the jettison bin, holding a hand over his mouth. He made it just in time.

Then he dropped onto the bunk, exhausted.

The reprieve gained by his elusive tactics must have been a long one. When Brad awoke he felt fresher than he had at any time since the engine compartment eruption. He had no way of knowing how long he had slept;

the secondary bus bar off which the ship's clocks operated had gone up in the initial blast when a section of the plate from the ruptured tube jacket had smashed through the junction box.

Evenly spaced *swooshing* sounds were emitting from the speaker. That, he realized, was what had awakened him. Someone was blowing into a mike to see if it was alive.

"SS Fleury, SS Fleury, SS Fleury," the sounds were suddenly exchanged for words—Altman's.

Brad swung his legs out of the bunk and stood swaying, rubbing a hand over his chafed, bearded face.

The elongated blip was back on the radar screen—clear, close.

"Answer, Conally," the receiver barked.

Brad strode to the panel and looked out the direct-view port He had slept longer than he had at first suspected. The stellar trellis had shortened considerably. They were back in the neighborhood of fifteen degrees.

"Distress Regulation Four-Oh-Eight-Two," the speaker droned, "says that if a disabled ship don't answer by radio or visually within fifteen minutes after being called steadily, standby craft is to board it and may take immediate possession."

"What do you want, Altman?" Brad said resignedly into the mike.

Altman hissed irritably. "Conally, there's no sense in playing hide-'n-seek with the little power you've got left. Get off that damned piece of junk and come aboard."

"Go to hell."

"Listen! I'm tired of wasting time! If you don't...."

"I'll sign a release and shoot it over to you. That's all you need to clear you of rescue and standby responsibility. I'll keep my distress signal off until you get out of range."

"Uh-uh. It ain't as simple as that. I want your cargo. And I'm going to get it. Now let's be sensible. You know you don't have a chance."

"Maybe I've learned a few tricks."

The other snarled impatiently. "Okay, bright boy. I've had enough of this horseplay. I'm gonna let you see just the way things are.... Notice anything odd? Any peculiar noises aboard the Fleury?"

Brad cocked his head toward the stern. The complaining clanks and groans and off-beat thumpings maintained their steady rhythm. There were some new noises.

"I been listening to it get louder for the past three hours," Altman hinted.

Then Brad's ears picked it up—an erratic, excited *clackety-clack-clackety-clack*. He gasped.

Altman laughed. "That counter's setting up quite a sing-song, ain't it? I sorta think that pile might go *boom* in a few hours. But I'm hoping I can get your cargo aboard before then. You can come too if you want."

Brad swung swiftly and lurched for the passageway aft.

"Wish I was there to help you with the cad rod insertions," the laughing voice raced after him.

The dial on the forward side of the shielded bulkhead read Oh-Oh-point-Oh-Two-Four. He applied the figure to the adjacent graph and learned he could remain in the engine compartment for one minute and fourteen seconds, with a safety factor of ten per cent. In that period of time, he rationalized, he ought to be able to insert a sufficient number of cadmium control rods to bring the pile under control.

The counter clicked gratingly overhead as he undogged the hatch, swung it open and lunged into the steam-tormented acrid compartment.

He broke open the first locker and jerked the remaining three cad rods from their racks. Coughing and waving smoke from in front of his face, he swung open the door of the first reserve compartment.

It was empty!

The second reserve compartment was empty too, as were the two emergency compartments. Only three cadmium rods when he needed at least three dozen!

In a rapid dash around the pile block, he inserted the rods at spaced intervals in their slots. At least they would mean a few hours' grace. As he slid the last rod in he cursed himself and swore that if he ever commanded another ship he would not leave it unmanned at the dock—specifically if there was somebody like Altman berthed anywhere at the same spaceport.

The ruptured hypertube jacket, he wondered suddenly, not losing his count of seconds. It seemed unlikely now that it had let go as a result of defective material. He stepped to the flange that connected it with the stern bulkhead.

The tube, inactivated immediately after the blowout, was cold. He looked where his suspicions directed.... The aperture control valve had been readjusted! It had been displaced a full fifteen degrees on the topside of optimum power! A cunning setting—one that would trap and concentrate enough residual di-ions at normal power output to cut loose somewhere between the fifth and tenth jump.

He thought, too, of his transmitter that hadn't been powerful enough to reach farther than a couple of jumps since he had left spaceport. When, he asked himself, had Altman's radioman worked on it?

After he slammed the hatch and dogged it, he leaned against the thick metal for a long while. The *clack-clack* overhead was somewhat pacified. But it wouldn't remain that way long. He quelled the fear sensations that were racing through him and tried to think.

How long? How long had it been since Jim left? He was three jumps away a few hours ago—or was it longer than that?—and he still had seven to go or was it six? Had it been just a few hours ago, or was it days? He had slept some—twice, he believed—since then. But for how long? And if the tow ships did make it back in time, would they have spare rods?

He gave it up as a hopeless speculation and started back up the passageway, shoulders drooping.

Karoom!

The new sound reverberated through the agonized vessel and the bulkheads of the passageway shuddered in fanatic sympathy with it.

The deck shifted crazily beneath his feet and a port beam—the bulkhead and the rest of the ship following it—swung over to crash into his shoulder.

A stabbing pain shot up his arm as he slid down the tilting wall and landed in the right angle between the deck and the bulkhead.

Massaging the torn ligament in his arm, he sat up and swayed dizzily in resonance with the pendulum-like motion of the vessel. Then he struggled to his feet and stood upright—one foot planted at an angle against the deck and the other against the port bulkhead. Overhead was the corresponding juncture made by the ceiling plate and the starboard bulkhead.

Nausea welled as he tried to adjust to the new, perverted up and down references. He didn't have to wonder what had happened. The starboard gray coil that ran under the overheated converter, he knew, had finally shorted out. The port coil was still operating normally. He considered turning it off, but conceded it was better to struggle around in an apparently listing ship than to be wracked by the nausea of weightlessness.

Straddling the deck and port bulkhead, he waddled back to the hatchway, threw a leg over its edge and lifted himself into the control compartment, sliding down the floor to the port side. He worked his way to the control seat, readjusted its tilt and crawled in it.

Then he tore a strip out of his jacket and wrapped it around his shoulder as tightly as he could. The pressure eased the pain in his aching muscle.

The air gauge showed an almost normal Two-Nine-point-Three-Two pounds, sufficient oxygen content, and a satisfactory circulatory rate. He eagerly fished a cigarette from his jacket. He had earned it, he assured himself.

While he smoked he counted on the screen the amount of cargo that had spilled out when the loose crates had lurched with the vessel. Almost as fast as he counted it, the Cluster Queen swooped down on it and scooped it into her hatch.

Numbed, he found he could no longer react to the total disregard of his rights with any degree of excited resentment. He closed his eyes indifferently. Shuddering, he squeezed the cylinder of tobacco between his fingers without being aware of the action. The glowing end bent back and burned his knuckle.

Tossing the cigarette away, he realized suddenly his fight was futile. He couldn't possibly hold out until Jim returned, or in the hope that some other vessel would happen along. The pile, his arm, spillthrough, the Fleury threatening to break in two ... he enumerated all the factors.

If he went aboard the Cluster Queen now, Altman would at least give him passage to port. Any charges Brad would make would never hold up without substantiation. And Altman would see that he brought nothing with him that could back up the accusations. It would be just as easy for the crew of the Queen to prove that Brad Conally had conceived the whole weird account of assault and piracy as a means of winning back the cargo he was faced with losing.

He knew, however, that no matter what happened, he could kiss the Fleury goodbye. Altman would never allow it to reach port. There might be evidence aboard—perhaps evidence as simple as finger prints—to prove that Altman or one of his crew had tampered with the machinery.

Brad reached out to extend the gooseneck of the mike toward him.

But the stellar grid showing through the direct-view port was blotted out suddenly. He jerked his gaze to the scope. The Queen was overhead—almost within grappling distance!

He started to shout out, but at the same time brilliant hell exploded outside.

The Cluster Queen's jetwash raked across the upper bow of the Fleury, throwing its nose down and its tail up and over in a hateful, wrenching spin.

The spin continued, losing none of its neck-snapping vehemence, as the Queen burst off into space. The harness cut across Brad's aching arm and set up a new, rending torture. But his good arm shot out and found the forward belly jet lever.

With what mushily reacted like the last erg of energy in the normal drive converter tanks, the jet responded feebly. He nursed the power carefully, determined not to waste juice through overcorrection. Finally the Fleury steadied and resumed immobility of attitude.

"Sorry, Conally," Altman apologized with exaggerated concern. "But her majesty's acting up frisky-like. Can't seem to do much with her.... Maybe if you came aboard we might find some way to quiet her down. How about it?"

Brad bit his lips and tightened his good fist until fingernails knifed into the palm. "No, damn you!" he shouted with all the volume his lungs could muster.

He summoned all the spacewise epithets any stevedore or crewman had ever used, added a few he imagined no one had thought of before, and held them in abeyance until Altman would answer.

But no sound came out of the speaker.

The reason was apparent on the scope. A half dozen of the massive crates had crashed through the hull—this time out of hold number One, the massometer showed—and the Cluster Queen was on her way to take them aboard.

But he was more concerned with another complication. The red power utilization indicator of the good hypertube was in motion, swinging back to zero on its dial. He saw the flicker of the needle in the corner of his vision.

He checked the suspicion against the blips on the scope and obtained verification ... the outlines of the Queen and the crates were fuzzy, despite the fact they were still nearby spatially. The fuzziness could only result from the Fleury's being removed hyperspatially from that vicinity.

He had accidentally touched the hyperjet lever while applying normal power to correct the three-dimensional spin. Which way had he moved it? Had he gone further into hyperspace? Or had he fallen further down the descending node toward spillthrough?

Studying sensations in his body for an indication of abnormal pain, he stared abruptly out the view port. The twisting pain was there—inside his chest. The star lines were short.

He swore and scowled at his luck.

Then, as the pain intensified, he grasped the lever of the hyperjet again and thrust it forward. The tube sputtered feebly, came on full force for a second, sputtered again and was silent.

He jerked the lever back and forth on the forward side of neutral and rammed it desperately all the way forward. The tube coughed, grabbed once more for a moment, and sputtered out. He goosed it four more times, but only got two boosts as a result. Then he twisted it past the stop to the first emergency position. It wheezed, fired for two seconds and died.

Sweat forming in beads on his face, he ignored the pain in his shoulder and reached to the control column with his injured arm. He swung back the second safety stop bar out of the way and rammed the lever all the way forward.

The tube fired for another second, but that was all. He had used the last erg.

But how much time had he bought with his final means of retreat from the spillthrough trough? He checked the celestial crisscrosses.... Not much....

Altman? he wondered suddenly. Where was the Cluster Queen? It wasn't showing up on the scope any longer. Neither were the crates. Had he retrieved them and shoved off? Brad jiggled the scope's brilliance control, wondering whether it was faulty and was simply not registering the Queen.

An abrupt *thud*, coincident with a sharp jar throughout the ship and a sudden shifting of the pseudogravitational field almost to normal, brought him upright in his seat. He realized immediately what was happening.

He hadn't been able to pick up the Queen on the scope because it was too close to register as a blip separate from the central luminescence on the screen which was representative of the Fleury itself. Altman had maneuvered alongside, aligned the hatch flanges of the two ships and activated his magnetic grapples. The nearness of his grav coils had restored some of the Fleury's internal stability. He was preparing to board the

Fleury. He would be aboard within ten minutes.... It took that long to make minute adjustments in order to insure perfect superimposition of the flange surfaces.

Brad smiled grimly and unsnapped his harness with nervous fingers. If he could get into his suit in time, it would be simple to open a hatch aft and let the air spill from the Fleury. Then when Altman undogged the inner hatch of the Fleury's air lock, it would be sucked open violently and pull the skipper of the Cluster Queen into a vacuum. It would make a mess out of the air lock and the control compartment—but that would be advantageous. It would be evidence to prove at least that Altman had taken the initiative in boarding the Fleury without first dispatching his intention of doing so to the nearest port, as required by the law.

Brad planned that if he then found the Queen's locks dogged, he would temporarily close the Fleury's inner lock and fill the between-ships passage with normal pressure air so he would be able to open the Queen's hatches against the thirty-pound pressure in the other ship. After opening her hatches, he would leap back to the Fleury's inner hatch, release the single doglatch and let the vacuum suck all the air from the other ship too. He would immediately report the defensive action to Vega IV, borrow emergency cad rods from the Queen, prevent an internal pile blast aboard the Fleury and withdraw the crippled ship, together with its engine compartment evidence, to the node of the arc to await the arrival of investigators.

He clamped the helmet on his neck ring with a minute to spare as he reassured himself it was a perfect plan and had a reasonable chance to success. It was one too that required no physical exertion. He couldn't go through any rough stuff with his sprained arm.

Stiffening, he watched the first of the six doglatches on the hatch swing to the unlocked position. He moved over against the starboard bulkhead, well away from the hatch. He would have to get out of the suit again, and it would be a messy job if he were standing close to Altman when the vacuum went to work on him.

The final doglatch unsnapped. The hatch crashed open and he imagined he could almost hear the swoosh of escaping air.

Instead he heard a mocking voice over his audio.

"You were right, captain," the voice laughed.

"Who'd think Conally would try a trick like that?" Altman taunted, extending a spacesuit clad leg across the hatch ledge.

"You would and did.... He'll probably be right behind the hatch to the left there, boss."

Brad sprang forward.

But Altman turned suddenly in his direction and pointed a gun at Brad's stomach. It checked the attack. Brad backed away hopelessly.

"Okay," Altman jerked his head in the confines of the helmet, "go to work."

The crewman from the Queen stepped into the control cabin and walked toward the passageway aft while Altman held the gun on Brad.

"Think you can do it quick enough?" Altman asked the crewman. "Radiation, you know."

The crewman thrust the wide-mouthed gun above his shoulder where Altman could see it. "It'll just take one shot with this."

He disappeared down the passageway.

"Hell, captain," the voice sounded a minute later. "It's dead. He musta used up all his reserve juice in that last surge upward."

"Okay," Altman smiled—a weird, distorted smile as seen through the thick, rounded helmet. "Come on back." He looked at Brad. "So you can't pull away from the trough any longer? That's tough."

Brad wanted to say, Okay, Altman, I'll go aboard the Queen with you. But he didn't. He realized the plea would have been futile anyway as he watched the crewman rejoin Altman and heard the latter say: "Just think, Conally, you could have come aboard. I would have let you a while back. But you've made this thing too tough and gave my boys the chance to convince me we might have slipped up somewhere and you might be able to prove your side of the story."

The pair retreated to the air lock. Brad stood motionless, staring, not breathing.

"The pile'll hold," the crewman announced, "for another four hours, just about."

"Fine!" Altman exclaimed. "This junk'll slip through within an hour. That'll give us another three hours, at least, to get this stiff aboard the Queen and transfer cargo before she blows. Then we can mop up on whatever crates we've...."

But the air lock closed and the rest of his words were cut off.

If he could only get cleaned up before it came. If he could only enjoy the luxury of a bath, a shave, clean clothes. Brad laughed at the last item, wondering how clothes could be expected to remain clean if they were on someone making the spillthrough transition at coasting speed.

The Fleury lurched as the Queen cut loose and blasted away. Brad had watched the pressure gauge climb back to normal and was removing his helmet at the time. The ship's one-sided gravity field caught hold unexpectedly and he toppled to the deck rolling to the port bulkhead. His hurt shoulder rammed into metal and new pain knifed into existence as the heavy helmet clattered down and crashed against his head. The blow almost stunned him. But it left him with enough awareness to wish it *had* knocked him insensible—permanently insensible.

The scope showed more cargo had spilled out in the last lurch. The Queen started over toward the crates, but coasted past, turned and came back to take post spatially alongside the disabled craft. Already the other ship's outline was beginning to blur as the Fleury slipped away from her hyperspatially—down the arc.

Brad straddle-stepped on the deck and bulkhead to the control column and broke out his pack of cigarettes. Suddenly his feet left the deck. The port gray coil had gone out, he realized grimly, the current having dropped below the minimum requirements. For a moment he became concerned over weightlessness. Then he cut in the heel magna-grips of his suit and clanged onto the floor. At least, he wasn't confronted with a topsy-turvy ship any longer. He blew a cloud of smoke into the air and half-centered his attention on the scope. Two more crates had left the Fleury's holds. With the grav fields out on the ship, they did not take up orbit. They just floated away, at an almost imperceptible speed. But the Queen was still apparently not interested in picking them up. There would be plenty of time to do that; right now she must stick close to the Fleury spatially, Brad realized, so her instruments would indicate the moment the spillthrough to normal space occurred, so her crew could get to work.

As though hypnotized in inconsequential thought, he watched the crates slowly draw away. Almost incredibly expensive cargo. Cargo that Altman would surely not allow to go unrecovered. Even as booty, the crated equipment would bring every bit of what it was worth. But Altman would see that they were delivered—every one of them. A contract with West Cluster meant a good deal more than the face value of the one shipment of inter-calc banks.

Brad started and his face became alive with expression as a sudden realization drove home. It was followed almost immediately by a second jarring consideration. He tossed away the half-consumed cigarette.

It wasn't more than fifteen minutes later when he stood before the mike again.

"Altman," he called out.

Silence.

"Altman," he shouted louder.

"Go ahead and answer him, captain. Let's see what he has to say."

"You can't come aboard, Conally," Altman said finally.

"If you don't let me come aboard I'll slip through and be killed."

"Ain't that touching!"

"You mean you won't pick me up?"

"We'll pick you up all right—we wanna take what's left of you back to show how you died."

"It's like that then? You're going to kill me to get the cargo?"

"You're learning fast."

"Are you going to hook on to the Fleury and drag her in to port?"

"Are you nuts? The inspectors could easily find out that we worked her over before you left port.... What's the matter—got a sentimental attachment for that old crate?"

"Look, Altman...."

"Go to hell, Conally."

The background hum died out of the Fleury's receiver abruptly. Brad called twice. But there was no answer.

The SS Fleury was vibrant with the final pounding of its weakening vital parts.

Clank-sss, clank-sss, the coolant's safety valve hissed. *Boom ... boom,* the jangling piston rod pounded. The expanding metal plate added its *throom-throom* note.

The counter in the passageway *clackety-clacked* louder.

Their lines snapped by persistent tremors and lurches, more crates danced in the holds. Some of them eventually found their way to the gaping holes in the hull and, receiving a final, brief kick from jagged metal, floated lightly out into space.

In the scope of the Cluster Queen, the Fleury's outline became fuzzier.

With mounting groans, the tortured vessel wrenched violently as she slipped down the descending arc.

Then suddenly she was through—in normal space where stars shown with pinpoint brilliancy and where the celestial sphere was no longer a lazy, crazy crisscross of blurred lines.

The Cluster Queen started a wide hyperspatial turn, remaining spatially alongside the Fleury. She gathered speed as she swung around and straightened out and, with hyperjets blasting full force, plunged through the barrier in somewhat less time than a milli-second.

Ahead, the Fleury was picked up immediately on the scope. Like a hawk, the Queen closed the distance to the other trembling, silent ship.

Vega IV's spaceport was bathed in brilliant, blue-cast light from the magnificent sun.

The Cluster Queen was docked. A tractor kept itself busy rolling up the ramp into the ship and out again with huge crates that were apparently in somewhat poorer condition than when they left Arcturus II. An occasional splintered board jutted outward, held to its box only by loose nails.

Three men were next to the hold's hatch. They stood grouped about an elongated form that lay on the concrete apron, covered with a white square of linen. A spacesuit clad arm jutted out under one side of the covered square.

"We'll take you over to the office," Inspector Graham was saying. "You'll have to make out an affidavit, you know. We'll need a couple of your crewmen to verify it."

"Be glad to," Altman answered. "Any time you're ready."

"As soon as they pick up—Conally," the inspector looked down at the form.

"I don't understand it," Jim muttered, rubbing a thumb and forefinger over closed eyelids.

"*Maybe I've got a version that's easier to understand, Jim,*" the voice sounded forcefully from the direction of the hatch.

Inspector Graham and Altman spun around.

Jim didn't have to. He was facing the hatch.

Altman blanched; backed away; stopped, and held his ground.

"Brad!" Jim shouted unbelievingly and rushed forward to grasp his arms as the Fleury's skipper leaped off the side of the ramp. He was haggard but smiling.

"Who's this?" the inspector asked.

"This is Conally, the skipper of the Fleury," Jim explained jubilantly.

The inspector started, looked at the form on the apron, back at Brad, then at Altman.

"A trick!" Altman cried hoarsely. "I see it all, inspector. It's a damned trick! I've been roped in!"

He was putting on a rather good act, Brad thought. But he went along with his story anyway. As Brad unfolded the incidents of sabotage, threat, assault, refusal to assist, pirating cargo, plotting murder and disregard of Space Code Regulations, he watched Altman gain more control over himself.

"I realized about an hour before spillthrough," Brad was approaching the end of his account, "that the Fleury was no longer holding the spilled cargo in an orbit because its grav system wasn't working. Whatever crates broke free from the holds also broke free from the ship's system and were no longer being dragged down the descending node toward spillthrough. They were remaining stationary on the arc—where Altman was sure to pick them up.

"Your spacesuit, Jim, came in handy. Without it, nothing could have been done. I just filled it up with anything I could find—extra clothing, insulation from the ruptured tube, a few utensils. It didn't make any difference. The crew members who would handle the "body" would believe it felt as torn apart as any other space suited body that experienced spillthrough at a snail's pace.

"To add weight, I broke open a bin of hematite and poured about a hundred pounds or so of the stuff into the suit. I stirred it gently; got more hematite—red ocher, you know—and half-filled the helmet. We had enough control column oil left to wet it down rather thoroughly. The new mixture had a rich, dark-red color, just like I thought it would. I sloshed the goo around in the helmet so all the inner surface was coated with the mixture and with small bits of indistinguishable odds and ends; then I clamped the dome onto the suit and harnessed it in the pilot's seat.

"I put on my own helmet again, went aft and crawled into a half-busted crate. With the wrist propulsor, I jockeyed the thing out of the hold to make damned sure it would break free of the Fleury's system and wouldn't spill through with the ship. After I saw I was drifting off, I worked my way well into the bracing between the crate and the inter-calc unit so I couldn't be seen through the broken sections of the box.

"Sure enough—about three hours later, along comes grabbenheimer," he threw a thumb in Altman's direction, "with his grapples. I was able to squeeze out of the suit an hour or so after that. But I've been cramped up in that crate for two days, with only emergency rations."

Altman loosed a sarcastic laugh and turned to the inspector. "It's a damned clever trick, inspector!" he shouted. "I been grappled in on the scheme.... Like I said, I arrived when he was slipping through. I couldn't do anything to stop it. Naturally I wasn't going to let the cargo go to waste. Naturally I was going to bring back what I thought was his body—regulations say I gotta do that.

"But he knew for a couple of hours that I was coming in answer to his SOS. I had gotten a fix on the point where he was slipping through and he was certain I would follow the Fleury through to normal space, pick up his body and the cargo that was aboard and go back into hyper to get the rest of the cargo. He had time to make all those preparations. So he dreams up the scheme of hiding in with the cargo that's free in hyper and telling this story later. You see...."

Brad laughed. "Your tongue's working a little too fast, Altman. When I picked the crate I was going to ride in, I picked a very special one. The tractor's bringing it out now." He pointed to the ramp. Part of the space suit was visible through the splintered side of the box.

"That crate," he continued, "will carry more weight as evidence than the oaths of all your crewmen on a pile of Bibles stacked from here to Arcturus."

Altman frowned puzzledly.

Jim and the inspector looked at each other.

"Inside is one of West Cluster's integrator-calculator audio retention banks," Brad explained. "It took only ten minutes to hook leads from the bank input to the intercommunication jackbox in the hold and to switch it in on the radio voice system. With that setup, everything said on the voice radio afterward spilled over into the retention bank. The only reason why I held that final conversation with you was to get you to repeat what you had done and were planning."

Brad turned to Graham. "How about it inspector? Do you think the courts will see that we get compensation for the loss of the Fleury?"

"The least you'll get," Graham said, "is the Cluster Queen."

Brad looked up appraisingly at the massive vessel. "She ought to do as security on a loan to cover the purchase of two or three other spaceworthy freighters to go with her. Wouldn't you think so, Jim?—That'd make a nice nucleus for a fleet!"

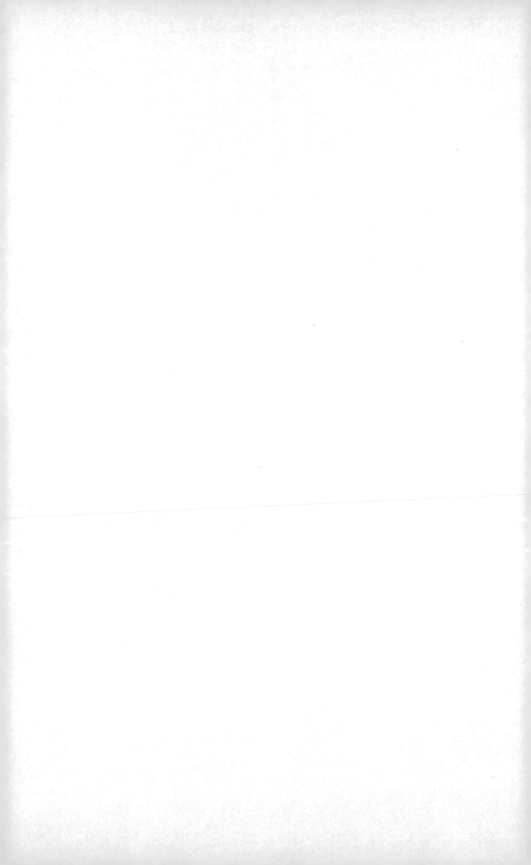